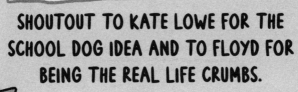

SHOUTOUT TO KATE LOWE FOR THE
SCHOOL DOG IDEA AND TO FLOYD FOR
BEING THE REAL LIFE CRUMBS.

B. D.

TO MY AMAZING WIFE MARTY AND
OUR LITTLE BELLY BOY.

J. L.

First published in the UK in 2023 by Nosy Crow Ltd
Wheat Wharf, 27a Shad Thames,
London, SE1 2XZ, UK

Nosy Crow Eireann Ltd
44 Orchard Grove, Kenmare,
Co Kerry, V93 FY22, Ireland

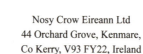

ISBN: 978 1 83994 936 4

A CIP catalogue record for this book will be available from the British Library.

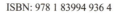

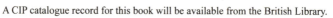

Printed and bound in Great Britain by Clays Ltd, Elcograf S.p.A.

Papers used by Nosy Crow are made from wood grown in sustainable forests.

FSC
www.fsc.org
MIX
Paper | Supporting
responsible forestry
FSC® C018072

1 3 5 7 9 10 8 6 4 2
www.nosycrow.com

IMPROVEMENTS

BANG, BANG, BANG.

The thudding from the corridor outside our classroom is so loud, I can barely concentrate on my daydreaming. I glance over at my best friend, Sam, and see he's covering up one ear with his right hand and scribbling down long-division answers with his left. My other friend, Jess, sits opposite, and I can tell she's not going to stand it for much longer.

"Ms Bottley!" she says to our teacher, not even bothering to put her hand up. "What's with all the racket?"

"Just some improvements taking place," Ms Bottley yells back from her desk. "I know it's distracting but please get on with your work."

I'm curious as to what's going on, so I get up, pretending to be going to the bin to sharpen my pencil even though the point could already pop a blimp. Mum always tells me I'm a "curious person". She says it explains why I'm always getting into trouble at school and that it's not my fault really.

I stand over the bin and peer through the window in the classroom door. I see Mr Greenford, the headteacher, picking up a framed certificate and beginning to hammer it on to the wall.

BRILLIANT SCHOOL
AWARD: 1998

1998? When even was that? Was it a school for dinosaurs? Why would he be putting that up? My curiosity is even stronger now.

"Ms Bottley," I shout over the hammering. "Can I go to the toilet, please?"

Ms Bottley would normally argue with me about how often I use the toilet, but she's too busy cutting out sugar paper for a poster that says:

CLASS 5B:
READING SUPERSTARS

"Yes, but be quick," she murmurs, with sticky tape clamped between her teeth.

Out in the corridor, I decide to get to the point.

"Mr Greenford!"

Mr Greenford, who has his back to me, screams like he's been jolted with an electric shock and accidentally hammers his hairy thumb.

"LENNY!" he yowls, clutching at his throbbing hand. "WHAT ARE YOU DOING OUT OF CLASS?"

"Toilet," I say. "What's with the certificates?"

I can now see he has lined the entire corridor with them. By the looks of things, the school won an award every year until the year I started. Weird.

"Why do you want to know?" he asks,

holding up his thumb. It's starting to go purple.

"Curious," I reply.

"Well, you know what curiosity did to the cat, don't you?" he grumbles.

"No, but I really want to know!" I say.

Before Mr Greenford can reply, Bill the caretaker galumphs down the corridor, his shoes squeaking like mad.

"Where have you been?" Mr Greenford moans. "I've had to do these myself and I think I've broken my thumb!"

"Don't blame me, blame whoever blocked the staffroom toilet," Bill shudders.

I can tell Mr Greenford isn't going to answer my question, but I still want to know what's happening. There's something not right with how nervous all the teachers are. Just this morning I saw Ms Patel from Year Two scrubbing the school sign with a toothbrush.

I linger around the corner and listen. At first it's just Bill moaning at Mr Greenford to tell the teachers they're not supposed

to flush memos down the loo, but then Mr Greenford takes over, his voice dropping.

"We need this school shipshape for the chief tomorrow."

Chief?! Like a police chief? Why would the police be coming to Fleurwood?

Back in the classroom, I stand by Ms Bottley's desk and announce the reason for the teachers' weirdness:

"THE POLICE ARE COMING TOMORROW!"

A murmur of excitement ripples across the room.

"Good!" says Amelia Kelly. "Maybe they're coming to arrest YOU!"

I stick my tongue out at her. She is the Joker to my

Batman, the Thanos to my Avengers, the … Amelia Kelly to my Lenny Lemmon.

I glance at Sam. He has turned as white as the whiteboard. Sam always thinks he's in trouble, even though he always follows the rules. Honestly, if Mr Greenford made up a rule that all kids called Sam had to dive into a vat of cow poo, he would do it. With a triple somersault.

"Can everyone calm down, please!" Ms Bottley says, standing up and giving me a "back to your seat" look.

"What Lenny probably heard is that a chief is coming tomorrow," she says. "But it is not a police chief, it's the school's chief executive."

Another murmur spreads across the class.

"It's nothing to worry about," says Ms Bottley, even though her face actually looks really worried. "It's just to see how brilliant you all are, OK? I will say this again: there is absolutely no need to worry."

THE NEXT MORNING

"I'm worried," says Sam as we line up on the playground outside school.

"Well, there's a surprise," chuckles Jess. "If there was an Olympics of Worrying, you'd take gold every time."

"No, he wouldn't," I say. "He'd be too

worried to go to the stadium."

"Listen," Sam snaps as we giggle. "I've been reading about these chief executives. Did you know they can close schools down?"

I gasp and my eyes go fuzzy. This could be my dream. No school! I'd spend all day doing fun stuff: playing, gaming. I'd never have to deal with Mr Greenford and his wacky rules ever again. No more tests, no more long division.

"Lenny!" Sam snaps his fingers in my face. "I know exactly what you're daydreaming about and it's not going to happen. All they'll do is send us to the nearest school."

"But the nearest school is—"

Sam nods, a grim expression falling across his face. "Birch Hill."

Oh no.

Jess nudges me, confused. "What's **BIRCH HILL?**"

I sometimes forget how new Jess is. She fits in with us so well, it feels like she's been around forever.

"**BIRCH HILL** is the worst school in town," says Sam. "No, scratch that – in the country. No, scratch that – in the

KNOWN UNIVERSE."

"What's so bad about it?" Jess asks.

Sam and I exchange a glance. We've heard the stories about Birch Hill. And we know the golden rule: if you see a kid in a Birch Hill uniform, **RUN**.

"At Birch Hill, the kids are in charge," says Sam.

Jess shrugs. "That sounds pretty cool."

Sam shakes his head gravely. "It isn't. It's chaos. Anyone considered not tough enough is terrorised."

Jess chuckles. "But I am tough."

"For Fleurwood, yes," says Sam. "But not Birch Hill. That place will eat you alive."

Jess glances over at me. Sam always exaggerates stuff like this, but not this time.

"We can't let the school get closed down," says Sam. "And that means none of your," he waves his hand at me, "adventures."

"What do you mean?" I say.

"Well, like when we were doing OLDEN DAYS SCHOOL and you thought it would be a good idea to bring in a RAT."

I roll my eyes. "You need to stop living in the past, Sam. It's going to be fine."

Sam shakes his head. "Why didn't your

dad tell you what's happening, anyway? He's a dinner lady here, isn't he?"

I sigh. "He's actually a lunchtime supervisor. And only on the little kids' playground. And they don't tell him any official school business."

Even if they did, he'd probably forget as soon as he got down to his lab in the basement and started trying to invent stuff. The other day he made a housework robot, but it went on a rampage through the neighbourhood and Mrs Hassan had to whack it with a frying pan until it fell into her pond and blew up.

A black car swishes into the car park on the other side of the playground. Mr Greenford sprints towards it and stands next to it, grinning. It must be the chief.

Our entire class is watching now. The door opens and a tall lady climbs out. Her hair is a cloud of fluffy white.

"She's scary," Parvati gasps.

I can't hear what Mr Greenford is saying, but I can see how the chief is staring over his shoulder, straight at us.

"Why is she looking at us?" Kieran Roscoe whispers.

"She's probably been warned about

Lenny," says Amelia Kelly snootily.

I want to stick my tongue out at her like I normally do, but the chief is still staring at us and I'm worried my tongue will shut down the entire school.

The classroom door opens, and Ms Bottley stands there. She seems to be dressed smarter than normal.

"OK, everyone inside," she says.

We all file in, but as my friends and I go to pass her, she holds out a hand.

Amelia Kelly shoots a look at us over her shoulder and almost bonks her head on a bookcase.

"Is everything all right?" I ask.

Ms Bottley waits until everyone else has gone inside before she speaks. "I'm sure it's fine," she says. "It's just Mr Greenford has asked that the three of you go up to the PE storage container on the school field. He's got a special job for you, apparently."

I frown, confused. "What special job?"

"He wouldn't say," replies Ms Bottley. "Just that it's important and will be a big help."

We look at each other. I can tell by Sam and Jess's faces they're unsure, but it looks like we have no choice.

"What do you think this is about?" says Jess as we make our way to the field.

"I don't know," says Sam. "But quite frankly, I could do without it. My stress levels are through the roof!"

"I don't know either," I say. "But if it's going to impress the chief, then it has to be worth it. No way do I want to go to Birch Hill."

Sam shudders at the mention of the name. "We'd better do the best job we can," he says.

THE IMPORTANT JOB

The PE storage container is a huge metal box at the far end of the school field, right by the back fence. We find the PE teacher, Ms Stack, already there. I gulp. Ms Stack is the scariest teacher in school. I remember when she taught us in Reception, Sam got so scared, he peed his pants. Then he got given replacement pants and peed those. He hates it when I tell that story.

Rumour has it, Ms Stack is a masked wrestler on the weekends, called the Dragon. I've seen photos and she does kind of look like her.

"Come along, you three," she barks.

I check Sam. He

seems nervous, but his trousers are dry. For now.

As we get closer, I notice Crumbs tied to a stake in the ground behind her. Crumbs is the Fleurwood school dog. Mr Greenford bought him to use as a reward: be good in school and you can pet Crumbs and walk him around the field and things like that. The only problem is, Crumbs is naughty. Very naughty. He's a Border

Collie. They're dogs that are used to move sheep around fields. And because there are no sheep, Crumbs will chase anything that looks even a little bit like one: poodles, fluffy white cats, little kids holding candyfloss. Last time I was outside Mr Greenford's office for yet another problem that wasn't my fault, I overheard him on the phone trying to sell Crumbs, but it seems like no one wants him.

Behind Crumbs, who has now started frantically racing around in a circle, I see there's another kid already inside the container. She comes running over to us. She's tiny so must be in Reception. She has her yellow hair in cute pigtails done up with pink bows and she's smiling.

"Hello!" I say. "What's your name?"

"Woof!" she yips back, then lunges at me and tries to sink her teeth into my leg.

"HEYYYYYY!"

"Gertie, no!" Ms Stack yells, pulling her away. I look at Gertie in alarm. Jess thinks it's hilarious.

"For the last time, you are not a dog!" says Ms Stack, leading the girl back into the container. She points at Crumbs. "That's a dog. You're a human." Gertie responds by barking.

Once she's calmed down, Ms Stack makes us stand in a line at the opening of the container. I make sure to get as far away from Gertie as I can and let her stand next to Jess. See how funny she finds it when she gets mauled.

Ms Stack paces around in front of us, her meaty hands clasped behind her back while Crumbs strains at the lead, whimpering.

"You have been sent here today to do a very important job," she booms. "Once a year, we have to count the PE stock. So that is what you will be doing today. You must enter the container and check how many footballs, how many basketballs, how many hockey sticks there are, and write the number down."

I put my hand up because I'm curious again.

"What is it, Lemmon?"

"How come a Reception kid is here if we're counting things? Can she do that?"

Ms Stack stares at me as if she's going to bite me too. "Don't worry about that, Lemmon. Concentrate on what you're doing and let me deal with Gertie."

This time Jess puts her hand up. Ms Stack groans.

"What is it, new girl?"

"Why is the dog here?"

Ms Stack shrugs. "I don't know. Because he'll track you down if you try to escape. Or something. Anyway, enough

of your questions."

She tosses clipboards at me, Sam and Jess and nods at all the equipment piled high in the container. We enter without another word. All around us are sacks of balls, nets, goalposts, hoops, rings, cones, and most of it is caked in mud.

"Are you serious?" Jess moans.

"Deadly." Ms Stack heaves herself into a deckchair in the entrance. "Now, come on. No time like the present."

I shuffle away from Gertie and pick up a big grey sack. It's much lighter than I thought it would be. Inside are a load of tiny white balls

with weird cones stuck on them. "What are these?" I ask, holding one up.

Ms Stack tuts and leans forward, squinting. "That's a shuttlecock for badminton."

I only understood three words in that sentence. "But there's loads of them!" I grumble.

"Better get counting then," Ms Stack snaps, then sits back in her creaky chair.

I can't believe this. Why do we need so many of these things? And why is it so important that we know how many there are? I would ask Ms Stack but she's already looking at me like she wants to shotput me across the field.

One … two … three … four.

My mind starts to wander. Like, if I were to drop this sack off the top of a skyscraper, how long would it take to hit the ground? I bet Sam knows. I look at him, jotting numbers down like it's the most important job in the world, but then another question pops into my mind. Why us? There are hundreds of kids at Fleurwood. What makes us so special?

CLUNK!

Jess throws a rounders bat down, earning a sharp glare

from Ms Stack.

"This is a conspiracy," she whispers.

"I don't even know what that means," I whisper back.

Jess tuts and steps closer to us, narrowly avoiding Gertie, who is sitting on the floor, chewing a relay baton.

"Do you really think Greenford picked us because we're the best ones for the job?" she says.

"Of course," says Sam, concentrating so hard that his face has gone all squinty and weird.

"What are you jabbering about over

there?" booms Ms Stack in her deep wrestler voice.

"We're discussing how to tackle the cricket wickets," Jess replies, before resuming her whispering. "They've put us in here so we're out of the way."

"What do you mean?" I say.

Jess rolls her eyes. She does that a lot. I think her brain goes quicker than mine and Sam's, and she gets annoyed waiting for us to catch up.

"I mean Greenford wants the school to look as good as possible in front of the chief, so he's sent the naughty kids, and dog, all

the way to the other side of the field."

Sam gasps like someone has just ripped a plaster off his scab. "I am NOT a naughty kid!"

I glance over at Ms Stack, but she is reading a book called *How to Stay Awake* and doesn't seem to be paying attention to us any more.

"But he sees me and Lenny as naughty kids, and you're our friend and kind of easily led," says Jess.

"I am NOT easily led!" Sam protests.

I rest a friendly hand on his shoulder. "You kind of are, though, Sam."

He sighs. "OK, maybe I am."

"I don't know about this, Jess," I say. "Mr Greenford is always going on about how I need to show some responsibility and blah, blah, blah, so maybe this is his way of giving me some?"

Jess growls under her breath. "Well then, why didn't he have you showing the chief around? Or doing something actually in the school?"

Hmm. Maybe she has a point.

"Seriously," Jess goes on. "If he could have sent us to school on the moon today, he would have."

Now, there's an idea. Imagine going to school on the moon. That would be fun. You could spend all day bouncing around. And your classmates would be aliens! I'd much rather sit next to a twenty-eyed purple blob monster from Uranus than Amelia Kelly.

"Lenny!" Jess hisses, clicking in my face. "Are you daydreaming again?"

"No," I say.

"He was daydreaming about Moon School," says Sam. He knows me too well.

Jess squeezes a football between her hands so hard, I'm worried she's going to pop it. "We need to escape," she whispers.

"No," says Sam. "I'm fine with being shut away. Do not cause a fuss."

I can see both sides. It's a bit like one of those old cartoons Dad watches, where the cat has an angel on one shoulder and a devil on the other and he can't decide which one to go with. Not that Jess is a devil. It's just she always really wants to do stuff, while Sam always really doesn't want to do stuff. But the more I think about it, the more obvious it becomes.

"I agree with Jess," I say.

"Of course you do," Sam whisper-shouts. "You two always gang up on me!"

"It's not like that!" I say. "Doesn't it annoy you that he's lumped you in with the naughty kids?"

Sam's eyes dart over to Gertie, who is staring at Crumbs outside the container and growling.

"Well, yes," he says. "But I'm hardly going to prove him wrong by being naughty, am I?"

Jess pokes Sam in the ribs, making him yelp. "Sam, there comes a time in your life when you must ask yourself if you want to be a pushover."

"Well, actually, yes I—"

"Because if you accept this now," Jess interrupts, "he's going to think you'll accept anything. Sure, today it's a PE container, but who knows what it might be next week? He could have you down in the cellar, fighting cellar monsters."

"There's no such thing as cellar monsters!" Sam protests.

"Do you want to take that chance?"

says Jess.

Sam closes his eyes and runs a hand down his face. "Even if I agree to this, do you even have a plan? How would we escape?"

"I was thinking one of us could create a diversion," I say. "Maybe pretend we need to throw up or something, then—"

"Hey!" a whisper comes from behind us. Jess is standing next to Ms Stack, who has fallen asleep in her deckchair.

"Oh," I say. "Well, come on then."

We tiptoe across the metal floor, and I wince every time it squeaks. Gertie follows behind, skittering across the container on all

fours, sending shuttlecocks flying.

We quietly file past Ms Stack, whose mouth is now hanging wide open, out on to the field. Sam looks like he's panicking, so I smile and give his arm a little squeeze to let

him know it's going to be OK. We're about

to make our way back across the field when:

RARARARARARARAR!

We spin round and see Crumbs straining at the lead, his eyes wild.

Jess desperately shushes him, but it doesn't work. It looks like Ms Stack is stirring in her chair.

Gertie darts from behind me and starts yanking at Crumbs's lead until she rips the spike out of the ground.

"Gertie, no!" I whisper, preparing for Crumbs to sprint away, but he stays still, staring into Gertie's eyes.

"Woof?" Gertie cocks her head. Crumbs lightly barks back, his tail wagging.

"Are they having a conversation?"

Sam gasps.

Gertie holds Crumbs's lead and guides him towards us.

"Whoa!" Jess holds up her hand. "We can't bring the dog."

She has a point. If we're sneaking back into school, the last thing we need with us is the most hyperactive dog in the world, but I can tell from the way Gertie is snarling at us that she isn't going to take no for an answer.

Besides, as I look down at Crumbs, with his mad boggly eyes, one ear sticking up and one pointing off to the side, and his tongue hanging out of his open mouth, I realise that the reason we've all been sent up here is that we're different. Well, he's different too.

"No," I say. "He belongs with us."

THE RETURN

Luckily, someone has left a door open, so we're able to get into school. It's quiet in the corridor. Normally you'd hear chatter from classes, but today it's so silent you'd think we'd broken in during the summer holidays. It's making me jumpy.

At the same time, I can't believe Mr Greenford would shut us away like that! He lied to us too! I don't know if I'm more nervous or angry. Maybe I'm both. I'm nangry.

"OK, we're back in," Sam whispers. "Now, what's the plan?"

"Isn't it obvious?" says Jess. "We find Mr Greenford and have it out with him!"

I can hear Sam gulp. He thinks of Mr Greenford as some sort of terrifying ogre, so I can tell he's not on board. I have to come up with a way that will keep them both happy.

"How about this?" I say. "We head back to

class and tell Ms Bottley the job is over. Then if Mr Greenford sees us, that's when we tell him we're on to him."

This seems to work, but first we have to sort out Crumbs and Gertie. We're close to the Reception classroom, so we open the door and, after convincing Gertie to hand over Crumbs's lead, get her inside. As I close the door, I hear the teacher say, "Gertie, how did you get back?" in a terrified voice.

Now we have to put Crumbs in his crate. It's just outside Mr Greenford's office, so that will probably be his first sign that something is up. Crumbs drags me across the hall so fast I have to run. Why did he walk nicely for Gertie and not me?

We stumble into the entrance hall to find Crumbs's crate missing. "Greenford must have hidden it," says Jess.

"So what are we going to do with him?" Sam cries. "We can't take him back to class!"

Crumbs raises his head and his nose twitches, like he's caught a scent. Suddenly the lead is yanked out of my hand and Crumbs becomes a black-and-white blur hurtling across the hall, straight for the

–OH NO!

THE STAFFROOM

I've only ever been to the staffroom a couple of times before, but it was never this clean. As soon as we burst inside, I can see what Crumbs is going for. On the table is a selection of delicious-looking cakes and pastries, glistening in the sunlight. I bet

Mr Greenford put them out for the chief.

"Crumbs, noooooo!" Sam screams, but it's too late. Crumbs leaps on to the table and begins his feast. There goes the cream horn! Goodbye, Belgian bun! Sayonara sponge cake! We scramble to stop him but he's too fast, and within seconds the cakes are gone.

Crumbs spins round and stares at us, his wild eyes even wilder and his icing-covered mouth hanging wide open.

"Oh my!" Sam yelps.

Crumbs jumps off the table and lands on one of the teachers' chairs. He grabs the cushion off it and violently shakes it, sending foam flying all over the place. I dive across to grab him, but he sees me in mid-air and escapes across the room.

"He's a fast one!" Jess yells. "Sam, you take the left, I'll take the right. Lenny, stay in the middle."

"I don't like thiiiiiis!" Sam cries.

I stand up as Sam and Jess take their positions on either side of the chairs, with me in the middle. Crumbs looks at us for a second, then spins round and turns a Fleurwood Primary tea towel into scrappy tatters. I've seen Crumbs be naughty before, but never this naughty. All the cakes must be giving him a sugar rush.

"On the count of three," says Jess, "we ambush him."

"Do we have to?" Sam whimpers.

"One … two…"

We dash across the staffroom and jump on to Crumbs, but he springs over us and we all crash together, landing in a heap next to the dishwasher. I get on to my knees just in time to see Crumbs leap on to the wall and pull down an "Outstanding Teachers" display to reveal the one underneath, which has a countdown to the summer holidays and a "difficult pupils" section, which for some reason has a photo of me under it.

But I don't have time to worry about that because Crumbs is running at top speed for the door, and he's smashed it open and someone in the entrance hall is screaming.

We scramble out to see Crumbs slowly approaching the chief, his head low, growling softly.

"Mr Greenford, are you aware there is a dog in your school?" she hoots.

"Y-yes, Ma'am," says Mr Greenford. He pulls a little plastic thing out of his pocket and presses it, making a clicking noise. "Here, Crumbs, there's a good boy."

But Crumbs isn't listening; he is still

creeping towards the chief. Why is he looking at her like that?

Wait a second. The chief's hair. It's white and curly. Like a sheep.

"Chief," I say. "You might want to step away, very slowly."

But it's too late. Crumbs is leaping. Crumbs is chasing.

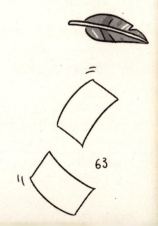

AFTERMATH

I'm sitting at home in front of the TV after tea, but I'm not really watching it. I'm thinking about what happened today: Crumbs chasing the chief into the stinky boys' toilets; the chief saying she's going to do a special week-long visit now. How am I going

to get us out of this one?

I'm trying to concentrate but the house is too noisy. Mum is in the other room doing her meditation chants, Dad is in the basement working on his inventions, and my annoying brother, Brandon, is in his room blasting his rubbish music. I clamp my hands over my ears and try to think, but it's useless. I'm getting distracted by the trailer for the new *Goo Heroes* game on the TV. It looks really good.

Wait a second. Of course. That's what I need to do. I need to make a trailer for the school! They always work on me, making me excited for things. Surely a trailer for Fleurwood will work on the chief!

The problem is, I don't have anything to make a trailer with. Dad has a video camera he made, but it already blew up once and I've got a feeling it will do it again.

But I know who does have one: Brandon. You see, Brandon is in a group. A terrible group called Snot Touch. They are always making rubbish videos for their songs. Their most recent one was called "Skool is for Losers" and it's somehow the worst one they've ever made. Anyway, they bought an old video camera between them, and I know

Brandon has it because I saw him earlier in the shed trying to film himself "freestyling".

Now, I could ask him if I can borrow it, but I know he'll just say no. He's that much of a poop-brained poopbrain. I'm going to have to be creative.

BORROWING

I sneak down the landing to Brandon's room. The door is shut, complete with a sign saying "Trespassers will be thrown into a volcano". I can tell he's inside because his rubbish music is still playing, like always.

The door flies open. "What are you doing

outside my room,
buttface?"

"I'm not the
buttface, you are,"
I shoot back. "And
how did you know
I was here?"

"I could smell you through the
door," says Brandon. "What do you want?"

I shrug. "Just hanging around. Free
country, isn't it?"

Brandon tuts and pinches my arm.

"OW!"

"Well, it's not a free landing," he growls.

"Now, get out of here before I take you down!" He points two fingers at his eyes, then one at me before slamming the door.

Ha! If he thinks I'm going to give up, he's got another think coming. And his thinks don't come very often. Rubbing my throbbing arm, I retreat to my room and wait for Brandon to come out. Maybe his dumb band has a show in a church hall or something. But I wait and wait, and he never surfaces. Not even to go to the toilet. Is he peeing into a bottle? I wouldn't be surprised.

It's getting late and my eyelids are drooping. How do you stay awake? What's the opposite of counting sheep? I don't want to think about sheep after what's happened, but now they're all I can think about, lovely … fluffy … yaaaaaaawn … sheep.

I wake with a jolt. Everything is black. I check my glow-in-the-dark clock. It's one in the morning. Wow. I don't think I've ever seen one in the morning before.

I want to crawl into bed, but this could be my only opportunity to take the camera. I rub my eyes and creep along the landing. There's no such thing as monsters, Lenny. Remember that. Well, except Brandon.

I hear Dad snoring. He's been extra-tired

since he got that job as a dinner lady on the little kids' playground.

I press my ear against Brandon's door. I can hear his heavy, sleepy breathing.

I gently push the door open a little and wait. His breathing is the same. I push it a little further. Still no change. I push it just enough so I can squeeze through and enter his room. I'm expecting it to be in darkness, but I notice a nightlight on his bedside table. I have to stop myself from laughing. What a baby. Still, at least it means I can see where I'm going.

I check on his chest of drawers, but there's no camera. His floor is covered in disgusting

pants and socks, and it smells like a pet shop. I pinch my nose to keep out the stench.

Brandon's wardrobe is at the far end of the room. I bet the camera is in there too. He seems to keep things in there that he doesn't want anyone else to know about. I remember finding love letters to a girl called Trixie Boo Boo once. Hahaha! Imagine being in love with someone called Trixie Boo Boo! What an idiot!

I creep as softly as I can over piles of crusty undies until I reach the wardrobe. Like with the bedroom door, I pull the wardrobe open centimetre by centimetre, until…

CLUNK!

"OOWW!"

Something heavy has landed on my foot and it really hurts!

"Huh?"

Oh no, is Brandon awake? I crouch behind his bed.

"Is that you, Trixie Boo Boo?" he slurs, which nearly makes me giggle. He must be talking in his sleep. He does that sometimes. I remember when we were in the car and he dropped off and started screaming, **"AAAARGH! THE DRAGON HAS STOLEN MY UNDERPANTS!"**

He swears we're all lying when we tell that story. I wish I'd recorded it.

I peer through the gloom and see the thing that landed on my foot. It's the camera! Yes! I give it a few seconds and wait for Brandon's breathing to go back to normal, then pick it up and crawl out on to the landing. When I'm back in my room, I stow the camera in my own wardrobe and cover it with a pile of clothes.

I climb back into bed, smiling. We are going to save the school.

FILMING

"Didn't know you were into antiques, Lenny," says Jess, examining the camera in the playground before the start of school.

"I'm not doing it." Sam folds his arms and tilts up his chin so he's looking at the sky, but he has to scrunch his eyes shut because of

the sun and he looks funny.

I put my hand on his shoulder. "Samuel. This could be our only chance to save the school. Do you want to end up at Birch Hill?"

He brings his face back down. "Of course not, but—"

"All we're going to do," I cut in, "is show the chief how good this school is."

"But how are we going to do that?" he asks.

"We film all the best bits and play it to her," I say. "Simple!"

Sam looks unsure, but I can tell I've got him

on board. He was having nightmares about Birch Hill last night, he told me.

"First up, all we need to do is get some kids saying, 'I love Fleurwood!'" I say. "Let's start with you."

I press the red button on the side and look through the screen, where a tiny Sam stares at me nervously.

"How am I supposed to say it?" he says.

"Just be natural!" I say. "Don't overthink!"

That was a ridiculous thing to say. Asking Sam not to overthink is like asking Crumbs not to chase things that look like sheep.

Sam shifts from side to side. "I, um, love

Fleurwood!" he says.

"OK, try that again, but this time smile," I say.

Sam sighs, then tries to smile, but his eyes still look terrified. "I flove Leurwood!"

Jess groans and barges him out of the way. "We're not trying to win an Oscar here." She smiles and holds two thumbs up. "I love Fleurwood!"

"Perfect!" Then I take some shots of the playground. There's the Year Four classes playing a game of tag. There's a group of Year Six kids sneaking in a quick game of football.

There's class 5A standing in a perfect line,
in perfect silence, waiting to be let inside.

Some of them are even reading! And not anything fun either! Maths textbooks!

If Mr Greenford called an assembly and told us 5A are a load of robots he made in a lab, I would not be a bit surprised.

"Hey!"

A sharp voice snaps me out of filming the most boring class in the world and I spin round. Amelia Kelly sticks her hand over the camera lens and I have no choice but to stop recording.

"What are you doing?"

"Flying to Mars in a rocket. What does it look like?" I say.

Amelia tuts and folds her arms. "I wish. Why are you filming the playground?"

"What's it to you, nosy?" says Jess, glowering.

Amelia scowls at Jess for a second, then turns back to me. "What are you planning? I heard you set that dog on the chief yesterday. Are you trying to get the school closed down completely? Well, I won't allow it!"

Other kids are staring at us now. I need to calm her down. I think about how Mum dealt with Brandon when he was ranting about her accidentally dyeing his best shirt pink. I relax and lower my voice.

"Listen, Amelia. We're not trying to get

the school closed. We're trying to save it."

Amelia barks a laugh. "And you're going to do it with that?" She points at Brandon's camera.

"Of course!" I say. "If we put together a little film showing all our best bits in one go, the chief will see what we're really about. Like a trailer. Does that make sense?"

Amelia looks at me, then Jess, then Sam. I can tell she likes him the most of the three of us, and the fact that he isn't doing his "help me" face seems to make her feel better.

"You're serious about this?" she says.

"Super serious."

"Because if I help you and it turns out to be some stupid joke, I am going to get you, Lenny Lemmon. Do you understand me?"

"Yes," I say. "Wait, what do you mean, get me?"

"I don't know yet," she says, her voice low and threatening. "But I will."

I glance at Sam, who now is doing his "help me" face.

"I promise it's not a joke," I say.

Amelia grabs the camera off me and points it at herself.

"My name is Amelia Margaret Kelly and I have been a pupil at Fleurwood Primary for

five years and nine months. Fleurwood is the place I learned to read and write and do long division. Every day I learn something new and it makes me really happy. When I learn something interesting, it makes me feel all warm and full like I've had a delicious meal. Mostly, it is a place I feel safe. Sure, some of my classmates are idiots, but they are a tiny minority."

"We can edit that part out," I whisper to Sam and Jess.

"I know I'm not the only person to feel this way," Amelia goes on. "This is our second home. All our friends are here. Please don't

take it away, Madam Chief. Thank you."

Amelia gently passes the camera back to me and I don't know what to say. I didn't know she could be so … not mean. Amelia wipes her eyes with the back of her hand, nods quickly, then turns her back on us.

"I've got to hand it to her," says Jess. "That was good."

The classroom door opens and Ms Bottley notices my camera straight away.

"I'm making a film," I explain.

Ms Bottley chuckles. "Not in school time, you're not. Off, please."

"OK," I say. "Hey, before I do, can I ask

if Fleurwood is the best school you've ever worked in?"

Ms Bottley sighs wearily. "It's the only school I've ever worked in."

I shut the camera off. It wasn't as good as Amelia's speech, but maybe there's something we can do with it.

THE CALL

Every day a different group is given the task of walking Crumbs around the school field. It used to be a reward for good behaviour, but now kids are rewarded by not having to walk him.

Today it was some Year Six kids,

but Crumbs would not take his eyes off us and kept dragging them over. So that's why we have him now. I'm holding his lead extra tight, but at least he's not running off anywhere.

The good news is, we've nearly finished filming. We got loads of good stuff: kids playing football, tag action shots, dinner ladies serving up platefuls of steaming food, even a nice long zoom on the school entrance.

"We should get the library in there," says Jess. "The chief's going to love it if she thinks we read books."

"I do read books," says Sam. "And anyway, we're not allowed inside unless it's raining."

"You and the rules, Sam!" moans Jess. "What are rules when the school is at stake? I've only just got used to this place; I can't move again!"

Sam sighs and I feel bad for him because I know how much he hates our adventures. He just wants a quiet life.

"But what about –" His eyes dart to Crumbs. He's so scared, he can't even say his name.

"Two of us will hold his lead this time," I say, nodding at Jess. "There's no way he can

escape. Besides, we'll be in and out in no time."

Sam nods. "OK, Lenny. But let's make it quick."

We head inside, along the corridor and into the library, both me and Jess gripping Crumbs's lead until our knuckles go white. It's a small room that smells like dust. Some of the books are probably older than my grandma. Carol and Ron Learn Arithmetic?! No thanks! I scoop up one of the newer-looking books and pretend to read it while Sam films me, making sure to cut out Crumbs, who is sniffing an atlas.

"OK, that's great. Can we go now?" says Sam, his fingers clasping at the sleeve of his jumper.

"One sec," I say. "Just let me find some books that aren't crumbling into dust so I can film them and we'll be..."

A shadow falls across the glass in the library door. It's an adult-sized shadow. It isn't Ms Bottley. It certainly isn't Mr Greenford.

Whoever it is has curly hair. Curly white hair.

"It's the chief!" I whisper-shout. "Hide!"

We scramble behind a shelf and sit on the floor, our backs pressed against the wood. Sam is breathing heavily, and I mouth at him to stop.

"Stop what?" he mouths back.

"Breathing!"

He looks at me like I'm crazy.

I hear the chief's voice as she walks into the library. "No, the dog is being kept away from me, thankfully."

Crumbs starts growling so I stroke his head. *Please be quiet, Crumbs. For the first time in your life, be quiet.*

The chief sits on one of the creaky chairs and lets out a soft groan. I peek through a gap in the shelves and see she's on the phone. She's only a metre away from us and I really wish Sam would stop breathing so loud.

"Oh, it's finished," she says.

Wait. What's finished?

"Finito, kaput," the chief goes on. "No hope for it whatsoever."

"Is she talking about the school?!" Sam mouths, his eyes wild. Crumbs growls again, this time louder.

"Hang on a second," she says, then goes quiet. I hear the creak of the chair as she leans forward.

We look at each other. Our faces are terrified, except Sam's, which is a mix of terrified and "I told you so".

Crumbs starts panting so I desperately hold his mouth closed, but it springs open and he starts licking me, thankfully not too loudly.

"Never mind. I thought I heard something," says the chief.

I breathe again. Maybe she's moved on.

"Yes, it's a shame, because I really did think

it had some life in it," the chief goes on. "But it's beyond repair."

She can't be talking about the school, can she? I strain to hear the other voice on the phone. It's muffled but I'm sure it says something like, "But what about the kids?"

"They'll just have to make alternative arrangements, won't they?" she snaps.

My stomach twists. She is talking about the school! She ends the call, gets up and leaves.

"What are we going to do?" Sam yelps while trying to stop Crumbs from climbing on to his head.

I grab Sam's hand, then Jess's. "We are going to make the greatest trailer the world has ever seen," I say. "It's our last hope."

Outside school, we watch everyone playing.
If only they knew what was about to happen.
Then they wouldn't be so happy. But come
on, this is no time to mope. We need action!

"We should go and film in the little kids'
playground," says Jess. "Make sure we get

the whole school."

"But we're not allowed to go down there!" says Sam.

He's right. As soon as you go up to Year Four, there's no return. The little kids' playground might as well be in a different country. Luckily though, it's just down a slope.

"Hey, it's fine," I say. "My dad's the dinner lady there, remember? As long as we're quick, we won't have any problems."

Gripping Crumbs's lead tight and making sure we're not being watched, I lead the crew down to the little kids' playground.

A ball rolls over to us and a boy with bowl

hair and thick glasses runs up to get it. He looks up at us and gasps.

"BIG KIDS!"

A scream zooms across the playground as a hundred little ones run away from us like we're a horde of zombies. It takes all my strength to hold Crumbs back and stop him chasing them.

"WE PROBABLY SHOULDN'T FILM THIS," Sam yells, a hand over one ear and the camera over the other.

I see Dad by the fence. He's waving me over, all panicky. That's weird. He's not the panicking type. When his inventions blow up, he just shrugs and chucks a bucket of water over them.

"Everything OK?" I ask him.

"No!" Dad yelps. "One of the kids has escaped!" He nods at a hole under the fence. "There's this girl who thinks she's a dog. She's dug her way out!"

Sam, Jess and I look at each other. "Gertie!" we say in unison.

"What are we going to do?" says Sam.

Dad pulls his phone out of his pocket. "Now is the perfect time to try out my patented Child Tracker. The radar on this bad boy can locate any child with a tracking device on them."

I sigh. "And does Gertie have a tracking device on her?"

Dad stares at his phone for a second, then blinks hard. "No."

"Right, so we'll have to think of something else," I say.

Dad gulps. "I can't lose a child! If Greenford finds out, I'm done for!"

"Don't worry, Lenny's weird dad," says Jess. "We'll find her."

"Will we?" says Sam, horrified.

But before I can decide whether it's a good idea, Crumbs slips free of his lead and ducks under the fence, disappearing down the road and round the corner.

"Oh no, not Crumbs as well!" I say, looking

down at my hand where the lead used to be.

Without another word, Jess gets down on her belly and squeezes through the gap.

"Come on," she says from the other side. "We need to find both of them. Crumbs I'm not so worried about, but if the chief finds out there's a kid missing, we're cooked."

Well, that does the trick. I get down and crawl through, and Sam, after chewing his thumbnail and going, "Ooh, I don't know," for ages, joins us.

"Don't be long," Dad says. "One lost kid is bad enough, let alone four!"

Sam has gone pale and shaky, so I give his

shoulder a squeeze to let him know it's all going to be fine. Maybe it is.

"She can't have gone far," says Jess.

"Yeah," I say, trying to sound hopeful for Sam. "She's only tiny and… Wait a second, what's that?"

There's a little side road next to our school and on the other side of it there is something small and pink lying on the pavement. We head over and I pick up a ribbon, exactly like the ones Gertie has in her hair.

"She must have gone this way," I say.

The side road leads to a much busier one. Turning left takes you into the town centre, whereas right goes into the countryside. We check around for any other signs, but there are no clues as to which way she might have gone. No sign of Crumbs either. Then again, with how fast he took off, he could be in Paris by now.

"Oh, this is hopeless," says Sam. "We're just going to have to go back and tell Mr Greenford."

"Who will be with the chief, who will close us down and ship us to Birch Hill?" I say.

"We've got to keep looking," Jess agrees. But if we go the wrong way, we will lose valuable time. We need help. We need ...

WOOF!

The bark echoes from further down the road. We exchange a look, then run.

ROUNDING UP

"Here!" A lady stands on her front lawn holding out a treat to Crumbs, who approaches slowly. We creep up behind him, being careful not to make a sound.

Centimetre by centimetre, Crumbs's nose gets closer to the treat, and I can tell the lady is ready to pounce. The problem is, Crumbs can tell too, because he snaps on to the treat like a hairy crocodile then turns and goes to sprint away. But **BLOOOSH!** He barges into Sam, sending the two of them tumbling down the sloping lawn into a bush. Me and Jess dive on top of them and I hook the lead back on to Crumbs's collar.

"OK," says Jess. "We've got Crumbs; now to get Gertie."

I think back to something I saw on TV once. It was a film about a super-clever dog that could track down missing criminals. All it would have to do is sniff something that

belonged to them. That's when I remember: Gertie's ribbon!

"Here, boy," I say, holding it in front of Crumb's snout. "Get the scent."

Crumbs takes off up the road towards town and I am once again being dragged like the dodgy exhaust pipe on Mum's car. He's determined to get us around this sharp corner.

RRUFFFF RUUUFF RUFFF!

When we get round there and see what is happening, we all scream. There is Gertie, standing in the middle of the road, barking at oncoming cars.

I call her name, but it's no good. Besides, she probably can't hear me over Crumbs's barking. He yanks at the lead, but I hold on tight. Sam holds it too and almost drops the camera.

Crumbs shakes his head really hard.

"Lenny!" Sam shrieks, but it's too late. Crumbs has pulled his head out of his collar.

He runs into the road, darting around cars, and nudges Gertie on the back of her legs, moving her bit by bit until she's out of the road and back to safety.

With the two of them on the pavement, I get Crumbs back on the lead and try to take them back to school, but Gertie stomps her foot and yells, "No!"

"She can talk?" says Jess.

Gertie grabs the lead off me and the two of them trot calmly back to school.

"Thanks, kids!" Dad says, as he fills in the last of Gertie's escape tunnel and covers it with a rock.

"Don't thank us, thank Crumbs!" I say.

Once we get him back in his crate, Sam holds up the camera and shows us the last footage. He must have switched the camera on when he fumbled it and recorded the whole thing.

"We're going to have to delete that," he says.

"Are you kidding me?" says Jess. "This is gold! You can show everyone that Crumbs is a good dog after all."

We look down at Crumbs in his crate, happily chewing on a stuffed pig toy. "Well, when you put it like that," says Sam.

I pat the camera. "Let's see what comes out in the edit."

THE TRAILER

A drawing of planet Earth.

MY VOICE: In a world of violence.

The same drawing but with BANG! scrawled over it.

MY VOICE: The only safe place is school.

The video of the outside of school comes on, with dramatic music in the background.

JESS: I love Fleurwood!

SAM: I flove Leurwood!

The video shows some library books.

MY VOICE: A place of education.

The video shows kids playing football.

MY VOICE: A place of sports.

The video shows a dinner lady plopping spaghetti on to a plate in slow motion.

MY VOICE: A place of culinary excellence.

We see Crumbs nudging Gertie out of traffic.

MY VOICE: A school whose dog is an ACTUAL HERO.

MY VOICE: And it's not just the kids. The staff love it so much, they don't even recognise other educational establishments.

MS BOTTLEY: It's the only school—

The screen quickly cuts to a photo of Mr Greenford.

MY VOICE: The only school. Fleurwood is the only school. And don't just take our word for it. Here is twenty-eight-time Star Learner, AMELIA KELLY.

From there, it goes to Amelia's speech, which is annoyingly brilliant.

"That's pretty good, isn't it?" I say to Sam and Jess. We've been working on it at my house for hours, taking it in turns to have a go at splicing all the videos together.

"If this doesn't save the school, nothing will," says Jess.

I hit save, then yank out the data stick and put it on the side, next to another one that must belong to Brandon.

"Tomorrow," I say.

THE BIG MOMENT

We're in the hall for assembly with Mr Greenford. The screen is down behind him, so he can show pictures while he talks. Today he's made the extra effort, with animations and sound effects. I can't concentrate on what he's saying, though.

I'm too busy waiting for my moment. The chief is sitting at the back, like a moody statue. Meanwhile, Crumbs is curled up next to Gertie at the front. Someone must have noticed that they seem to calm each other down and decided to keep them together.

I reach into my pocket and grip the data stick. I look at Sam. He's sweating even though it's not even hot. Jess gives me a determined nod.

"OK." Mr Greenford claps his hairy hands. "Now it's time for me to open the floor to you, just like we do every week. Ask me anything!"

A little hand goes up at the front.

"Yes, Lila?"

"If you could get ate by any animal, what would it be?"

Mr Greenford smiles, but I can tell he's not happy. "I meant any questions about school."

"I WOULD PICK A TYWANOSAUWAS WEX!"

"Any other questions?"

I put my hand up and lift my bum off the floor so I'm higher than everyone else, but he doesn't pick me and instead goes for Rupert from 5A, who asks some boring question about whether he can start studying high school maths because regular maths isn't challenging enough for him.

Mr Greenford goes around another couple of times, but I can tell he's avoiding me. He needs to pick me or our plan goes out of the window. I nudge Sam.

"Put your hand up," I whisper.

His eyeballs bug out like I've just asked him

to run round the hall clucking like a chicken.
"What? Why?"

"Because you're the sensible one of us
three so you have the best chance of being
picked," I mutter back. Ms Bottley
sees me talking and gives me a
"shut up" look.

"Come on," I whisper
through the corner of
my mouth. "Do you
want to save the
school or not?"

Sam sighs, closes
his eyes and puts

his hand up.

"Ah," says Mr Greenford. "We'll take one from Sam."

"Um…" Sam's mouth flaps open and shut like a fish, before he turns and looks at me. "Lenny has a question."

Mr Greenford's face falls like a lollipop man on an icy road. "Oh."

Here goes. Jess gives my shoulder a supportive thump and I get up.

"Lenny," Ms Bottley whispers, but I pretend I can't hear her and make my way to the front of the hall.

Wow. That's a lot of people. The whole

school, plus the chief. The only time kids get to come up here is when they're getting a Star Learner award and I never win those.

"It's not really a question," I say to Mr Greenford, whose head has turned so purple it looks like it might pop. "But I do have something important I want to say."

I move over to the computer by the screen and plug in the data stick.

"Lenny, what are

you doing?" Mr Greenford growls, storming after me and yanking the stick back out.

"We made a film," I say. "Me, Sam and Jess. It's all about how Fleurwood's the best school in the world. We wanted the chief to see it."

I look at the chief. She is staring at Mr Greenford and nodding ever so slightly, almost like a gust of wind has caught her head.

"OK!" says Mr Greenford, in a bit too jolly a voice. "I always encourage extracurricular creativity, so let's watch Lenny, Sam and Jess's film!" He motions for me to sit back down and starts putting the stick back into the computer.

Jess puts her hand on the floor in front of me. Sam adds his, and I put mine on top. Here we go. Our last chance to save the school.

The screen goes black.

BBYYAAAOOOWWWW

Wait. That's not how our trailer starts. But it sounds familiar.

The screen bursts into life to reveal Brandon's terrible group dancing around in front of a grotty brick wall. The middle one, who Brandon calls Dogmeat, but whose name is actually Jeremy, looms over the camera and screams,

"SCHOOOOOL IS FOR LOOOOOOOSEERRRRRRRRS!"

Mr Greenford sprints across to the computer, falls over his own legs, does a roll and yanks the stick out of the computer while the whole school laughs, cheers and whoops, and Crumbs barks.

I'm yanked from behind and Amelia Kelly's face is right in front of mine. "You promised me this wasn't a joke," she hisses.

"It wasn't! I must have picked up the wrong data stick!"

"Well, thanks to your data stick, we're finished!" Amelia growls. "We're going to Birch Hill! I might as well shave my head and get face tattoos!"

"YOU THREE!" Mr Greenford roars. "UP HERE NOW!"

I release myself from Amelia's grip and stand up. Sam is sweating even more now and looks like he's going to puke.

We stand at the front of the room. The laughing and cheering has stopped. Everyone knows they're about to witness a good old-fashioned telling-off.

"I suppose you think this is all a joke, don't you?" Mr Greenford yells. "Well, I'm not laughing!"

"Mr Greenford—" I say.

"Don't interrupt," he shouts. He's so angry a glob of spittle flies from his lips and hits a Reception kid in the front row, who starts crying. "You fooled me into thinking you had done a good thing for once in your entire time at this school. Well, I will not be fooled again. Let's see how many pranks you three pull when you're

SUSPENDED!"

Sam gasps and his knees buckle, and me and Jess have to hold him up.

"Please, Mr Greenford," I say. "This isn't Sam or Jess's fault. We really did make a film, but I brought the wrong data stick in. That's my brother Brandon's rubbish band."

"I know it's Brandon's rubbish band," Mr Greenford says. "He came to this school too, remember? Every morning I wake up and thank the universe there are no more Lemmons after you."

"Wait!" Sam yelps.

Mr Greenford looks stunned that Sam has spoken up.

"We really did make a film," he says, then with trembling hands reaches into his pocket and pulls out another data stick, one I don't recognise.

I don't wait for permission. I take the stick and put it in the computer. Our trailer starts up.

"Sam!" I whisper, squeezing his shoulder. "How did you do that?"

Sam takes a wobbly breath. "While I was on the computer last night, I set it up so the save would automatically go to my dad's email and downloaded it. Just in case something went wrong."

Good old Sam. Always prepared.

"You the MAN, Sam," says Jess, thumping his shoulder.

When the trailer is over, a huge round of applause goes across the hall. I look over at Amelia Kelly, but she's staring at the floor, like she's embarrassed. That's when I notice the chief stand up and walk towards us. The applause has died down and it's silent again.

"Hello, everyone," she says, looking out at the hall. "My name is Barbara and I am the Chief Executive of the schools in this trust. First of all, I'd like to congratulate these young people on their wonderful film."

Another round of applause.

"Secondly, I'd like to say that I was never

planning on closing down the school."

A low murmur ripples across the room and Mr Greenford waves his arms to get everyone to be quiet.

"Wait a second," Jess says. "We heard you saying 'It's finished. Finito, kaput.' When we were hiding in the library."

Barbara laughs a warm chuckle. "It's true, I did say that. I was on the phone to my husband. And I was talking about my car. It broke down yesterday morning."

Oh.

"Hang on a sec," says Jess, waggling her finger at the chief. "If that's true, then how come we heard your so-called husband say, 'What about the children?' and you said something like, 'They'll have to make alternative arrangements'?"

Barbara laughs again. "You kids have good hearing, I'll give you that. My husband was referring to our children. Well, they're adults, really. I'd told them they could borrow my car to drive to a concert."

That stumps even Jess.

"So you're definitely not closing the school down?" I ask her.

The chief shakes her head. "I'm just here to see if everything is going well. And while

I'm here, I might as well tell you what I think."

I look over at Mr Greenford. He's chewing his fingernails like they're made of Skittles.

"The standard of teaching at this school is good and the facilities are also good," she says. "Having said that, I'm not sure about safety standards when it seems that your unruly dog has been corralling a child off a busy road."

Crumbs jumps up and lets out a little yip.

"Whoops," I say.

"So all in all, I would say that Fleurwood Primary is … pretty decent."

Mr Greenford throws his hands into the air.

"PRETTY DECENT! YES!"

Sam nudges me. "Lenny, I seem to have forgotten what words mean. Is that good?"

I put my arm around my old friend and give him a squeeze. "It means you don't have to worry about Birch Hill any more."

Sam nods with a little smile, then faints.

It's Friday afternoon and we're leaving school. Me, Sam and Jess are walking together like we always do. We pass Crumbs, on his tenth lap of the field with Gertie and showing no signs of stopping. What a dog.

"This week feels like it's lasted three years," says Sam wearily.

We pass the chief standing at the bus stop and I give her a wave. She smiles and waves back.

Meanwhile, Mr Greenford is excitedly shaking all the parents' hands and boasting about how Fleurwood is "pretty decent".

I take a satisfied breath. Fleurwood might not be the best school in the world, but it's my school and I wouldn't

have it any other way. Actually, I would. I'd have it loads of other ways. I suppose what I'm trying to say is, it could always be worse.

"You know," says Jess. "I kind of enjoyed making that movie."

"Me too," I say. "It was exciting."

An idea starts to form in my head and Sam must be able to tell because he's staring at me.

"Lenny," he says in a warning tone.

"In fact, maybe I want to do it again!" I say.

"No," says Sam.

I rub my hands together. "Yeeees. We could make our own movie. A proper one."

"No, we couldn't," says Sam.

"Sure we could," says Jess. "How about an action movie, with explosions?"

"NO!" Sam yells.

"Better yet," I say. "How about a horror movie?!"

"**YEEEES!**" Jess says, leaning over to give me a **HIGH-FIVE**.

"No, Lenny. No, Jessica. I will not make a horror movie," says Sam. "I refuse. And this time I'm putting my foot down."

We'll see, Sam. We'll see.